The Longest Strongest Thread

INBAL LEITNER

Scallywag Press Ltd
LONDON

This suitcase is SO HEAVY.

The Longest
Strongest Thread

A book to share from
Scallywag Press

For my grandma, with love

First published in Great Britain in 2020
by Scallywag Press Ltd, 10 Sutherland Row, London SW1V 4JT

This paperback edition published in 2021

Text and illustration copyright © Inbal Leitner, 2020
The rights of Inbal Leitner to be identified as the author and illustrator
of this work have been asserted by her in accordance with the
Copyright, Designs and Patents Act, 1988

Printed on FSC paper in China by Toppan Leefung

001

British Library Cataloguing in Publication Data available
ISBN 978-1-912650-61-3

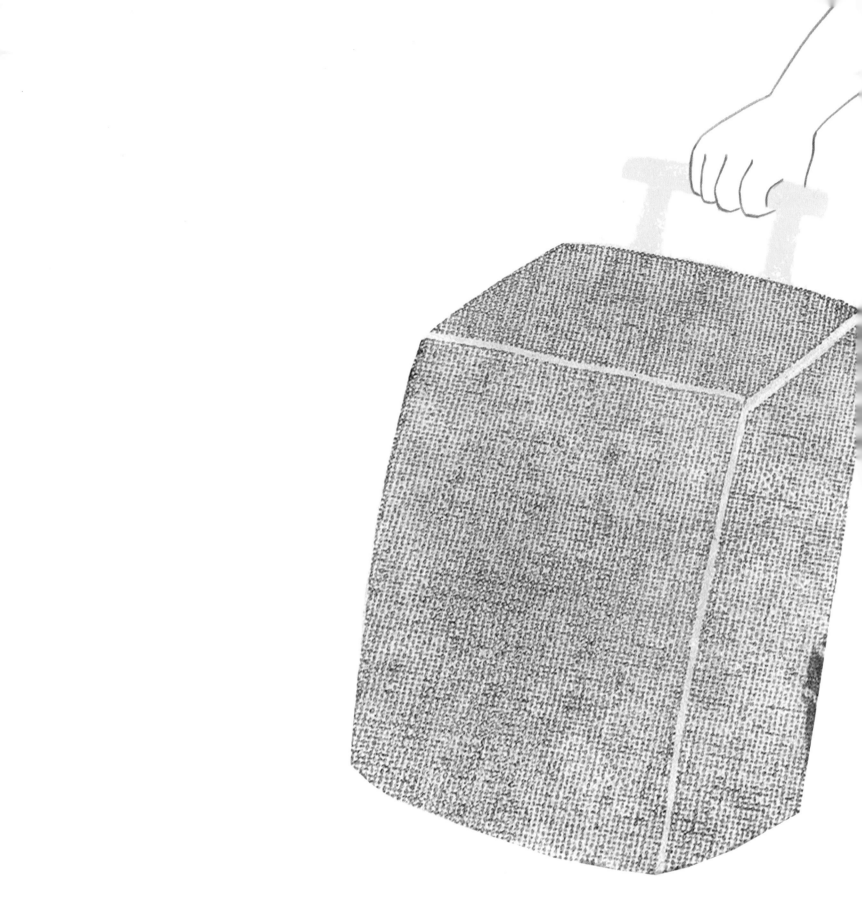

I think it has everything I'll need in my new home,
where the lakes freeze in winter.
We are flying there soon.

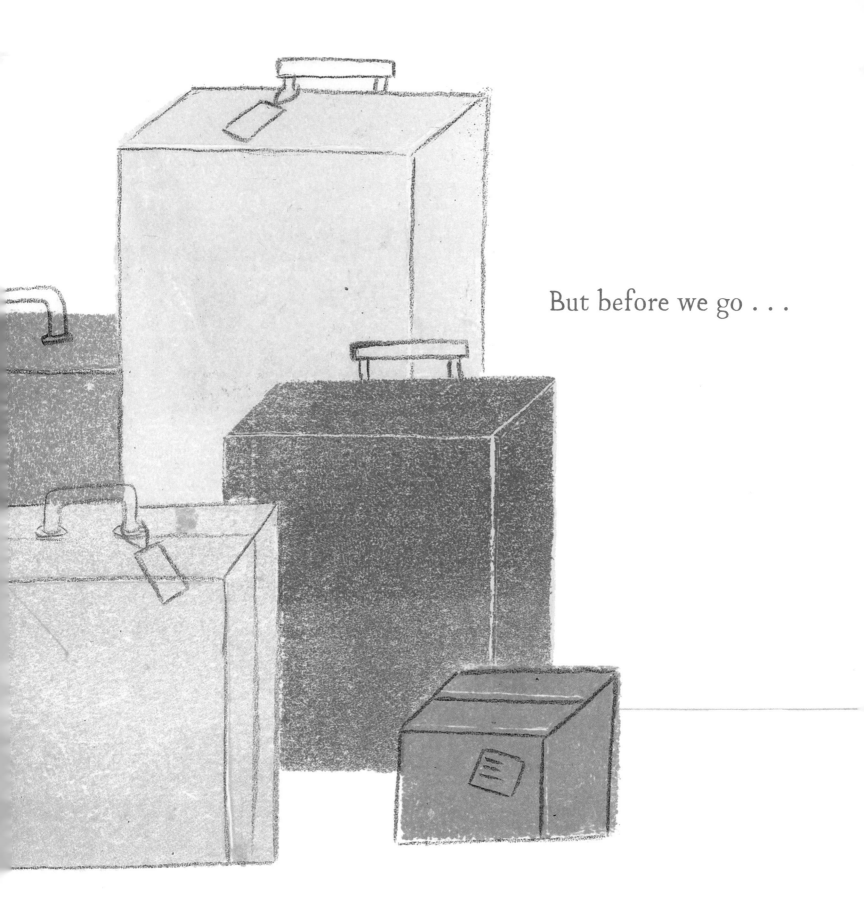

But before we go . . .

. . . I am visiting my Grandma to say goodbye.
I wish she could come too.

She is staying here where it is warm
and she has her sewing studio.

I LOVE Grandma's studio.

I help her choose
soft, warm fabric

and the strongest
blue thread.

My new home is very far away
from Grandma's studio.

I must draw her a map so she can find me . . .

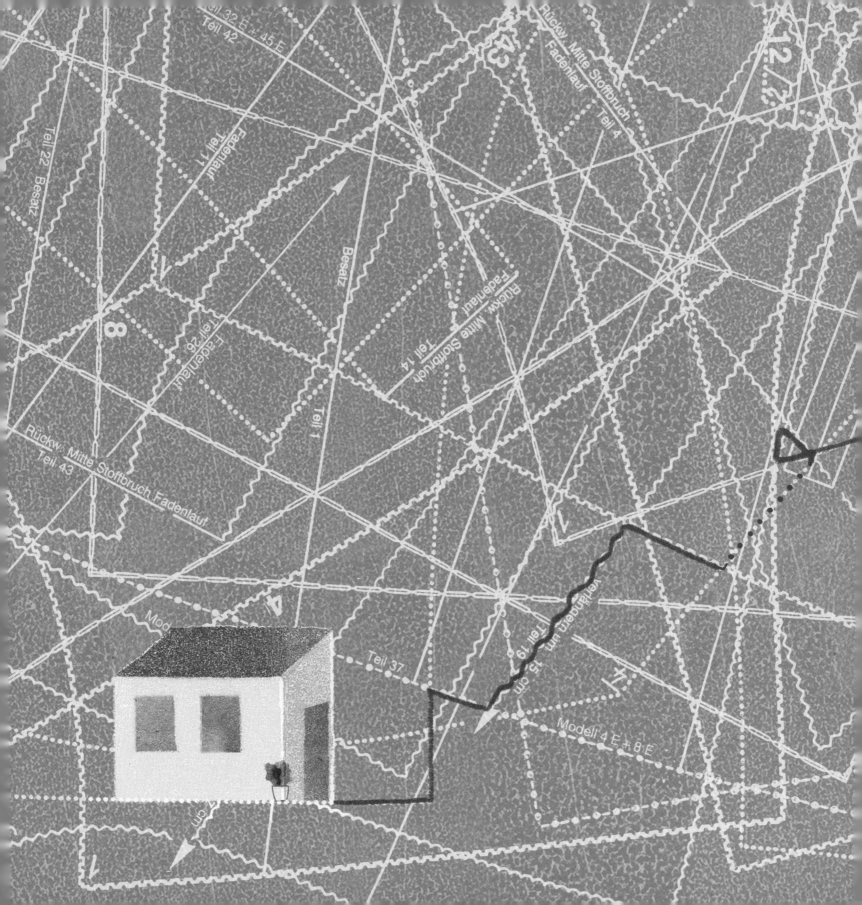

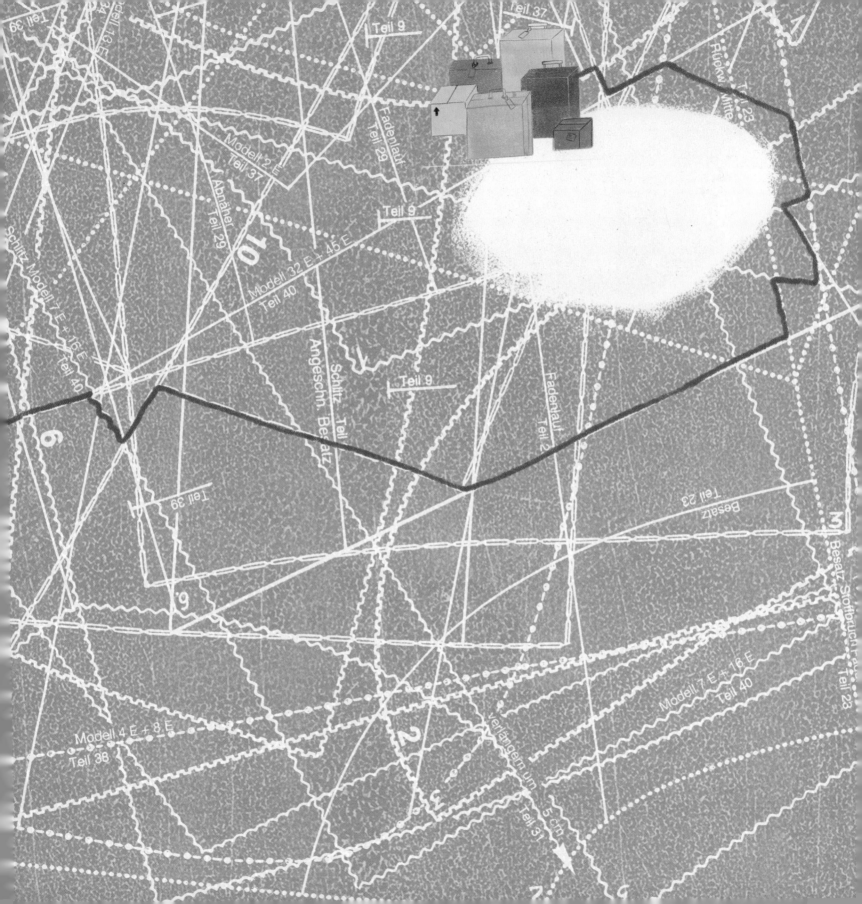

But even if she
knows where I am,

Grandma can't walk
all the way to my
new home.

So I am making her an aeroplane she can fly with.

If only there was an enormous pin magnet
I could use to pull her to me whenever I want.

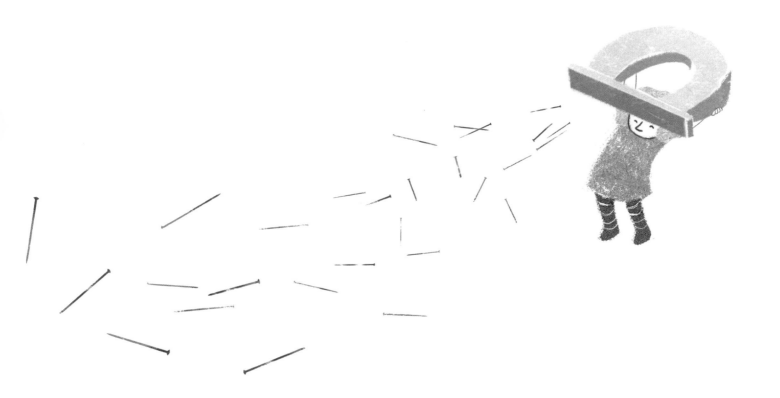

Grandma says I mustn't worry
that my new home is so very far away.

She says we two have the longest, strongest thread
in the whole world.

I love Grandma,

and Grandma
loves me.

We don't want to say goodbye.

But she promises me that when winter comes
and the lakes freeze . . .

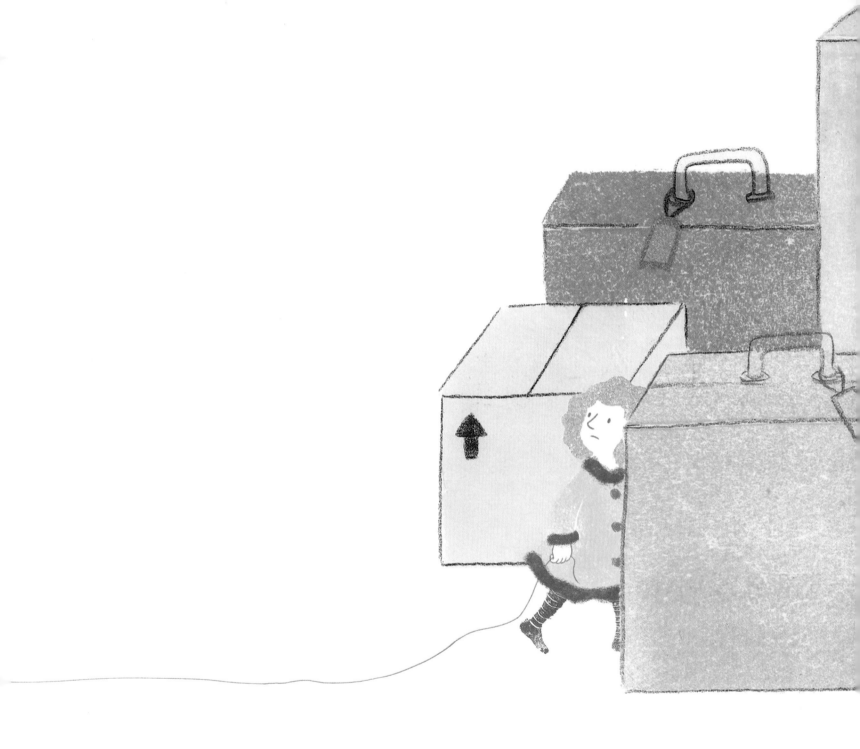

. . . she will surely use the map I gave her
and fly all the way to find me.